The House of Forever

Also from Raven Electrick Ink

Sporty Spec: Games of the Fantastic
Cinema Spec: Tales of Hollywood and Fantasy
Retro Spec: Tales of Fantasy and Nostalgia
Jack-o'-Spec: Tales of Halloween and Fantasy
Spec-tacular: Fantasy Favorites from Raven Electrick Ink

The House of Forever

Selected Poems

Samantha Henderson

Raven Electrick Ink

First edition, October 2012

ISBN: 978-0-9819643-5-5

Raven Electrick Ink
Los Angeles, California
http://ravenelectrick.com
comments@ravenelectrick.com

Contents

Introduction

Time, especially time travel, is a frequent theme in speculative fiction and poetry. When I first read Samantha Henderson's poetry, I noticed that much of it bends time—not time travel per se, but time-folding, time-collapsing, and time-conflating, so that now becomes then, and then becomes now. Time-bending is such an integral feature of Samantha's poetic worldview that she hadn't really noticed it until I mentioned it to her. It's simply the poetic air that she breathes.

In the moving poem "Cabazon," the prehistoric past, in the form of concrete dinosaurs and Neanderthals, meets the lonely present, as a bereaved man chats with an alien and contemplates the end of the world:

> The alien was leaning
> against the Northeast leg; he walked by without
>   acknowledgement
> (nowhere else to go) and climbed inside the tail
> to the tiny store where they sold plastic dinosaurs,
> fossilized dinosaur dung,
> and postcards.

"The Miracle of the Gulls, 1848" finds futuristic "gears, half metal, half crystal" within the frontier world of plague-stricken farmers:

> Jared was a good boy, he meant no blasphemy
> When he picked up the dying angel choking on the shore,
> Held it gently in rough hands while it coughed, and died,
> With a mechanical crick of the neck. When it was quite still
> He probed, tore apart the bloodless breast. Seventy years
> before a word like "robot": still, he understood.

"Victory Garden" tells of Arthur's knights and World War II; "What Scuttles" juxtaposes zombie cinema and Pharaoh's Egypt; "After the Crash" invokes the Brontë sisters in deep space.

Thus, we present *The House of Forever*, 21 poems, nine never before published, connecting past, present, and future, each a tapestry of life sewn with the unraveling threads of time.

Karen A. Romanko
Los Angeles, California
October 2012

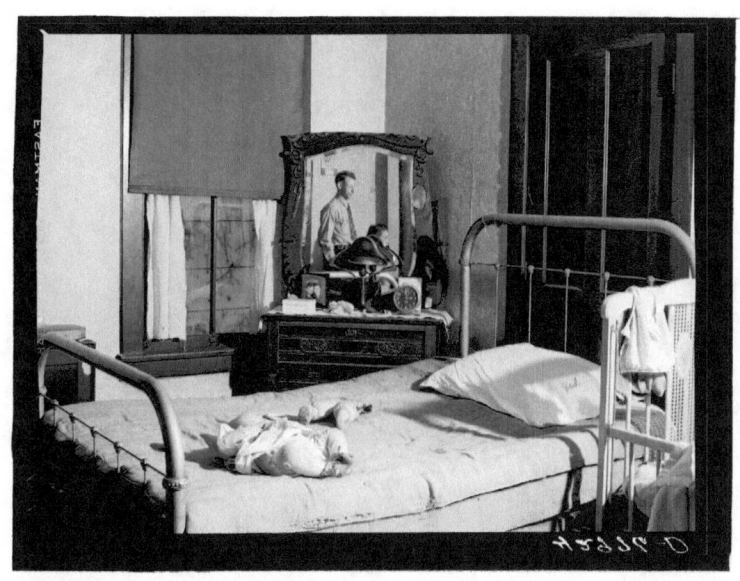

Family Living in the "Crackerbox" Slum Tenement in Beaver Falls, Pennsylvania
Library of Congress, Prints & Photographs Division, FSA/OWI Collection,
LC-USF34-042976-D (b&w film neg.)

Crackerbox (1941)
Beaver Falls, PA

Jack Delano's forehead is captured, inset like a cabochon
in the silver-peeling hand mirror, in that moment,
when he turned and saw the shot. How his heart
must have caught in his throat, to see them so revealed,
sideways fragile, and their portrait grinning bravely back,
the dresser holds so much—clock, linen, shears—
of the beating heart of life:

Did *he*, unconscious of it, think of Jim's legbroke boy?
Did *she* carry sorrow like an egg inside her?
The child, so deep asleep that sleep itself is in love,
that sleeping child—did he become
sinner, sagebrush prophet, pilot,
dry bones beside the road, my uncle,
wreathed in my mind in pipe-smoke?

This room would smell of dust and lavender
and the babe's soiled clouts, and the perfumed places
in a woman's neck, the leather of a working man,
a whiff of soured milk, and in the summer,
the privies below or just outside.

This room would taste of the secret spaces
an old house hides behind nailed doors
and forgotten crevasses, and holds tight
to itself. And wallpaper glue, and the rot
that winter coaxes.

Veritas Was a Maid in the House of Forever

Veritas was a maid in the House of Forever
Which the weekend guests never understood.
Kitchen maid,
Laundry maid,
Who sees your stained sheets, and the gristle you found
Buried in the meat at dinner,
And spat discreetly into your napkin.
Finite, they find her,
Dangling at the end of the Butcher Boy's rope,
Her head at an unnatural angle
(Like a toucan's beak),
After she slits the stolen canvases in Milady's
                Milord's
                The Butcher Boy's
                Chamber.
The next morning comes the knock at the servants' entrance:
Her cousin
Her sister
Her niece
Her aunt
Chapped to the elbows,
And pitiable thin.

What Scuttles

Who says what scuttles is not blessed?
They knew that called the scarab holy:
as a body is given to women to be washed,
and in turn delivered to the soil,
so these little brothers, these sweet sisters
engage in their sacred work—a tender plucking of the flesh.
Watch—your horror films: one with zombies;
or the Grand Guignol frisson of stepping into an open grave;
or the piled victims of last month's engineered virus;
your torture porn, your grue-fests.
The fantastic artificers, that make the unreal appear,
and take pride in their work, like Pharaoh's embalmers,
craft putrification and gravedirt just so—
but the maggots in their jars, ready to be scattered for show:
they will dine, and process, and excrete,
making all one, and don't mind
that it's all play and pretense—
it's in their innocence that they remain hallowed.

When They Woke

Gamma Quad was sealed when they woke,
coughing stasis-gel out their lungs
and staring at their metamorphosed
comrades, their own changeling features,
twisted out of woof and warp,
in horror.

There are no records
of what happened next,
only a red smear they left
uncleaned on the canopy,
to remember.

Of Beta and Epsilon: nothing—
twisted tin for all they knew, or severed
portstrings caressing the ethereal side
of those indifferent, implacable cargo doors.
But after the frenzy, when the survivors,

only partially maimed, calmed and decided
upon another path than slaughter, that play,
was the way to greet death, as belabored
air recycles wheezed on, slower and slower—

They embraced their deformities as fine-wrought masks,
each finding Loki, or the Dog-Faced-Boy,
or bird-headed demons, or Indra Descending,
her heart held in her hand, in the polished,
useless surfaces set oblique

in every corridor.

And at the very end of time,
all the heroes wanted to dance
down at Medusa's in the dark.

Mouth Feel
(For Joe Haldeman)

In the early adolescence of the Space Age
I rolled marshmallow blobs in Tang,
the bright, sour crystals sweet
to my untutored mouth.

Watching the fatal double plume
fork on the screen, I taste
beneath the salt of ready grief
my childhood invention:
the sweet, the sour.

Hepatocellular Cancer, Stage Four

On the beach across the street from the liquor store that's down the road
     from the clinic,
A bicycle rusts, bent almost in half,
Useless even to the beggars
And wild children who beg for candy in almost perfect English.
Five steps beyond: nothing below your feet but air, more air,
Air scrubbed clean by salt,
And salt water, blue as a blind kitten's eyes,
Deep as the world. Turn around, make careful note,
Of the stripped hills, a woman rummaging in a stained steel barrel,
A strip of red fabric caught on a doorsill and slapping the ground,
And tell me why I should not fall backwards.

In the Lenten season they smear ashes on your face,
Dry and gritty beneath the priest's rough fingers,
And you are told that dust thou art, and to dust thou shalt etcetera.
But they are wrong, we are, at best, smears,
Water with a little dirt to make it interesting. You see this at the end,
When your legs mottle yellow and your ankles swell, and your fingers

Are tight as sausages, and you become
Merely a way for water to walk about.

Around my ankle, taut
With parasite water, I've roped the rusty bicycle.
I'll gift myself to the careful crabs,
Not rot, but dissolve
A little fall, a cold shock,
Exit,
Stage four.

15

Cabazon

He stopped at Hadley's to get her dates
(because she liked the Medjools, although tray after tray
piled, crystallized, in the refrigerator)
and made it to the aisle before he remembered.

Drove on the service street
past the tribal-owned Denny's,
past the casino, sprouting like a strange neon flower,
to Cabazon, where the world cracks open,
and concrete dinosaurs guard the alluvial plain,
while the bunch-backed clouds, thick with rain and apocalyptic promise,
brim over San Gorgonio
trapping the light of a dying sun.

He stopped at Hadley's to get her licorice
(before he remembered that she was gone),
chopped into red cubes, too sweet to chew,
but sucked until your mouth is raw.

The brontosaurus was pink in the dusk,
and now he saw its eyes glowed yellow with discontent,
while the T. rex's were ruby,
with a jolly, predatory look.

He stopped at Hadley's to get her pistachios,
shells opened, begging like the beaks of baby birds
(before he remembered that she was gone, forever),
she'd crack them in her mouth.

The alien was leaning
against the Northeast leg; he walked by without acknowledgement
(nowhere else to go) and climbed inside the tail
to the tiny store where they sold plastic dinosaurs,
fossilized dinosaur dung,
and postcards.
It smelled, as he remembered, of old, cold concrete,
and a sign reminded him that it was,
in actuality,
an apatosaurus.

The heads, rough-sculpted in the bumpy walls,
of early man still looked down,
like grisly trophies,
looking, as always, faintly reproachful.

(The Tyrannosaurus's name is Mr. Rex, he read on a flyspecked card,
but he'd always called him "Bob" in bedtime stories,
Bob, and his improbably apatosaurus mother,
who lived in a little house behind the bushes
behind the back garden,
behind her bedroom.)

"Rickets," said the concrete Neanderthal. "Lack of sun, hence
        Vitamin D,
due to climactic conditions,
resulting from the Deluge. That is all: no bowed legs,
no brow ridges,
deny it as you will, brother."

"Seeding," said Peking Man. "Extraterrestrial seeding."
(Outside the alien shifts his weight and smiles.)

"Angels brought us in spaceships, and taught us masonry and geometry,
demons live in the Hollow Earth."

Lucy's big ape eyes brimmed,
and he leaned close to hear her whisper:
I know what's it's like, Mr. Man; I have lost one too.
And he remembered, PBS blaring in the background,
the phrase: *the female's footprints,*
deeply indented on one side, indicate she carried a burden on her hip,
perhaps a small child.

The alien was leaning against the Southeast leg.
"Of course she's not dead," he said, under an avuncular fedora (aliens
always wear fedoras like Bogart). "We took her, for purposes beyond
          your mortal ken.
We always do: no one dies. Not here, not your daughter,
not your mother,
not your wife. We will return her, one day,
when she has served her purpose. Even now, as the sun explodes,
rest assured we will scoop you up;
your Anasazi roommate
will tell you wonderful stories."

The apatosaurus was watching them
with disappointed, yellow eyes.
"Canst thou draw out Leviathan with a hook?" it said.
"Or his tongue with a cord which thou lettest down?
Wilt thou play with him as with a bird?
Or will thou bind him for thy maidens?"

"Wouldn't dream of it," he said.

"You've been practicing that for a while, haven't you?" said the alien.

But the dinosaur was sulking.

He drove east, towards the false waterfalls of the Cities of the Plain.
Behind him rain, before him fire,
dates, licorice, and pistachios on the passenger seat,
to seed the new, clean-burned land.

Hero

I've taken away your magic boots,
your enchanted sword,
your ring of invisibility.

I've taken away your talking cat,
your princess,
and her clever maid.

Look, down in the crumbly depths
of your knapsack, there—you forgot
your grandfather's fountain pen.
Fill it with my blood,
and write history.

Hungry: Some Ghost Stories

Some of the following is true.

The Ghosts in the Kitchen

They gather in the kitchen sometimes; I can feel their cold bellies pressing into my back as I stir the soup, the risotto, curious as they strain to look over my shoulder. There are three: short; middling; and tall; like a vaudeville comedy act. When it's very hot and I have to use the stove I close my eyes and wish for their marble-smooth coolness, but they never come then.

I don't think they were people who lived in this house. Sometimes I don't think they were people at all. There's not that much personality to them—only curiosity.

The other place they gather is the bedroom, right in the middle of the old chest of drawers that was damaged during the London blitz. One, two, three. Perhaps that's where they're from: England of the 1940s, killed in the bombing. On rationing, and that's why they're so obsessed with the kitchen; they're hungry.

Do you have any ghosts? What do you feed them?

The Ghost on the Porch

He's standing on the porch, and I'm inside, staring at him through the rippled old glass of the living room window. His hands are in his pockets, and he looks out to the street, his back to me. It's evening, and I'm stripping thick paint off the redwood built-ins. My hands are burning from the chemicals; I have to be careful not to rub my eyes.

Later I hear from my neighbor that the son of this house married the daughter of her house when he returned from duty during World

War II. An airman, he survived overseas service, came home, married the girl next door and was killed in a training accident a few months after the wedding.

She also tells me he made the Adirondack chair that's stored in the garage.

I remember that his clothing has a look of the 1940s about it, but I don't know if that's a detail I've added in after hearing about the airman.

I am, by nature, a liar after all.

The neighbor died last year; she beat breast cancer twice but the third time got her. During one of her treatments she lost all her hair. She came over to try on some suits I was getting rid of: they were black and plain and sharp and with her shiny clean head and lean old body and slightly pointed ears she looked like a very modern, anime vampire. She looked wonderful.

I had a vivid dream about her about a year later: she'd opened up a bed and breakfast in the Land of the Dead. I don't know if that counts as a ghost.

What ghost have you made out of whole cloth?

My Uncle's Ghost

On June 17, 1958, several temporary struts reinforcing the Second Narrows Bridge in Vancouver, British Columbia failed. A number of workers were killed when they fell into the water below.

My uncle was one of them.

My uncle was also the engineer who had designed the struts, and it was determined at the time that it was an error in his calculations that caused the failure.

At the time of the accident my grandfather, in his bed in Sydney, woke to see his son standing at the foot of the bed, reaching out to him.

I don't know if that story was true or one of the many, many stories that grew like wildflowers around the stories of my uncle's death: how he walked onto the bridge at the last minute; how he dreamed about it the night before; how he knew his figures were off and told his bosses but they ignored him. Each story is a ghost in itself.

He was the only son, the golden boy. We create ghosts because we're hungry for them, not the other way round.

What ghosts have you spawned on your family, your children, your generations, yourself?

The Dog

Painting the children's room and accustomed to dogs, I step over the coiled figure of a black lab in the center of the room amid a cluster of paint cans and crumpled newspapers. The roller is on the wall before I realize I don't have a black lab. I roll on the thick cottage white and don't turn around because I know what I'll see. Paint can. Newspaper. Nothing else. The hair on the back of my neck prickles. I paint.

Much later my husband has transferred the home movies of the original owners to video and there he is: a black lab frisking beneath the fig tree in the back yard. The tree in the shaky black and white images is a spindly thing; now it's enormous, with a hollow trunk we're going to have to fill someday—it's eighty years later, after all. A few years ago my daughters found a family of possums living in the hollow, babies all pink and fetal, with hair like bristles poking out of their soft-looking skin, the mother all curved teeth like a mouthful of splinters. My dogs would pluck them like ripe avocados, and I pen them up until the possums leave.

Will you forgive yourself?

Eclipse

I get up early in the morning to see totality, the moon orange as a bruise, and find my neighbor in his front yard watching it as well. I don't know these neighbors, in an immense, beaten-up craftsman with its neatly raked yard, very well; there's a married couple with assorted adult children that come and go. I don't recognize this one, but he smiles and nods at me before turning back to the sky, and I think sometime before we must have met; perhaps I drove by and waved as he weeded the river-rock constructs in the front yard.

We watch companionably as the Earth's shadow passes, and then I hear him say, "'pop.'"

"What?" I say.

"There's a point when the moon turns into a ball, do you see it? It doesn't look flat anymore. It's three-dimensional. And it kind of goes 'pop.'"

I squint at the moon. He's right; it's round as a marble.

"You're right," I say, and there's no response. I turn to look, and he's gone. There are no lights on in the neighbor's house, no sound of a closing door. The air smells burnt, as if the moon is an ember.

I look for him in the front yard, but the man lifting river-smooth rocks isn't him. I think about asking but the subject never comes up.

Who lives with you, breathing your exhaled breath, eating the smoke of your sacrifices?

The Mini-Van

When I shut the door and glance in the rear view mirror, in that millisecond before the light goes off, I see someone sitting in the back seat. It's a little girl, with two blonde braids, I think.

How's this—she was killed in a car crash and the metal from that car was salvaged and melted and used in my Honda Odyssey and somehow she's bound to the metal or...

...I parked for a while at the place she was killed and her spirit just kind of moved in, or...

...it's an illusion made by the shadows cast by seat and belt and headrest, or...

...she's one of the possible ghosts that cluster around our children; every time they come home safe the wraiths of those potential deaths we fear every waking minute—the car skidding out of control, the serial killer lurking around the corner—cluster around them, invisible but we see them, we crave them, we eat them. A boy is dragged purple from the bottom of a pool; he gasps, he lives, but that branch of time where he didn't glows severed, like those Kirlian photographs of cut leaves—there he died and haunts us. And so, over and over, until the ghosts that never were multiply between us, blood of our blood, flesh of our flesh, and we feed....

My mother-in-law sat in the passenger seat for months after she died. I miss her very much. Sometimes she comes into the kitchen. They gather in the kitchen sometimes....

The Passion

We buried him past midnight,
(After the women fell asleep from crying,
Their veils sticky with tears)
Simon Peter and Matthew
And the Canaanite, and me,
At the crossroads, like a vampire
With the Bear, and the Scales, and the Serpent overhead.
Four of us, three clusters of stars,
Two women asleep, their mouths dry and open,
And him, stiff in linen.
I counted, over and over:
Four, three, two, one, to keep myself from screaming.
When it was done, and the soil smoothed over,
We turned away to prepare for the miracle.
Halfway down the road, the light shone out, cold, like moonlight,
And I knew it then, what we would see before we turned back.
He hovered, dangling like Judas, the earth cast back,
Like something monstrous had hatched,
Smiled, and our hearts were pierced by roses.

The Bear and the Snake bowed to him,
And the Scales sank down,
And we crept home, shamed,
Leaving to the sleeping women the first miracle
Since we had betrayed the second.
Four, three, two, one,
To keep from going mad.

Reptile Brain

On your next visit to the Zoo
(The kids begged you there, perhaps, or it was your turn to chaperone
the 5th grade Field Trip, or maybe you had visions
of popcorn on a fall day, and camel rides,
and innocent apes instead of masturbating bonobos),
When you tire of watching the elephants
Rocking back and forth in despair;
Or the polar bear in 98 degree heat,
His coat yellowed, and the lump of ice in his pool a mockery;
When you've seen the sea lions at their twice-a-day feeding,
Jumping and posing for fish in the shit-tinged
10,000 cubic feet of water,
Then go, thou, to the Reptile House,
Spare a glance for the lizards and the tortoises,
For they were old when your kind wobbled upright
on the sunburned savanna,
But pass them quickly and seek out the snakes.
It might be, if you watch them long enough,
The Burmese python looped upon her branch,
The coral snake a puddle of ivory, jet, and dull rubies,
The cobra with Buddha's mark upon his hood,
The gopher with his checkerboard belly,
That you understand they do not care about you, your overdraft,
Your mortgage or your cellulite or grace by redemption.
They know your ambient temperature,
With a pink flicker they taste your pheromones,
They see the serpent coiled around your brainstem,
woven into your cerebellum,
Embedded in your hypothalamus.

You might realize,
with the stink of the monkey house still in your nostrils:
They are wiser than you.
They are what you have been.
They are what you will become.

Autopsy/Mother Volcano

Autopsy

Beneath it all, her bones are made of copper,
hollow like pipes—a friendly color; that's why I remember.
Nothing of flesh inside her, nothing so plastic-wet:
zinc-strung nerves and sheets of tin where fascia should be.
Instead of lungs, a triple-loped bag filled with yellow granules,
and the stench from the throat of the volcano
whose child she was.

Mother Volcano

She is a cyst
bursting with dry, yellow matter.

Her sulfurous bones
become her children, sometimes to be consumed.

Like the Air, You Exist in Layers

Birds school high in chilly air,
and near the rock the wind stills,
sun-warm. Orange lichen crusts
the stone hump, and mica glitters
in ice-ground hollows
like coins in a suppliant's bowl.
Beneath that, the fine-grained matrix
Every shade of grey.
Beneath that, the ground
Continuously births rusty quartz.
Beneath the rotted log, a snake is sleeping.
Between two stones, a burrow.

Like the air, you exist in layers:
Cold enough to pierce lung-flesh;
Swift, insinuating as the Gulf Stream;
Sluggish and heavy-hot.

Like ink, you bleed
from page to page.
Leaving a backwards
Lemonade stain.

Every Thirty Years on Cygnus 5

How still the day seems without the wind
and hot, as if the air were pregnant, waiting...

Some go mad the day it stops:
not the young, not their first time.
It's 30 years later, when they feel it die,
and although they knew it would happen; knew
about the triple witching hour of flare, orbit, and dew point; knew
it happened three decades ago, will happen hence, still—
you know the ones: they chatter too loud, but their eyes are glazing
over, they are too still, like the air, like they try to hide
inside its torpidity, before they lash out,
running down the cliff-mazes, howling.
It's dangerous to stop them; you hope
their feet are sure; you hope
some kind angel guides them down.

How still the day seems without the wind
and hot, as if the air were pregnant, waiting
for something stillborn to drop from its belly
so it can move again.

The Miracle of the Gulls, 1848

There are those who will say that this was one of the natural courses of events, that there was no miracle in it. Let that be as it may, we esteemed it as a blessing from the hand of God; miracle or no miracle, we believe that God had a hand in it, and it does not matter particularly whether strangers believe or not.

Discourse by Elder Orson Pratt
Delivered in the Tabernacle,
Salt Lake City, Sunday Afternoon, June 20th 1880

Deep beneath the brine at the edge of the Great Salt Lake is a layer as
       telling

as the stratum of charcoal the Iceni left underneath London
or the trash heap under the ruins of Jericho:

a dusting of very small
gears, half metal, half crystal

you'd think it was fossilized shells
or the carapaces of tiny insects

Jared was a good boy, but his faith was shaken sore
(he admitted years later, only a little shamefaced)
and you can hardly blame him: for who expected
the sight of a multitude of tiny demons—
Mormon Crickets, they called them later, but he had to wonder—
blackening the sky with a clap and a thump,

eating anything green: paint, Sister's overskirt,
and the wheat in the ear, hard fought for,

Jared was a good boy, but he never expected angels,
small and white, in the guise of gulls,
coming down ungainly from Heaven,
and devouring tiny black bodies, until full to bursting,
they flew to the edge of the Lake,
and vomited them up, only to return,

and take bellyful after bellyful
until the plague was gone, the crop saved,
and New Jerusalem safe in Utah.

Jared was a good boy, but he needed
The evidence of his own eyes; went to the slush
salt shore to see the bodies. Picked one up; it fouled his hand,
with a smear of grease and (could it be) (oil?)
Poked it; with a sigh and a whirr it fell apart,
looked like the parts of a train, but tiny, toylike,
the blue sheen of metal.

Jared was a good boy, he meant no blasphemy
When he picked up the dying angel choking on the shore,
Held it gently in rough hands while it coughed, and died,
With a mechanical crick of the neck. When it was quite still
He probed, tore apart the bloodless breast. Seventy years
before a word like "robot:" still, he understood.
Here, in his hands, madness—
there, in the fields, where pragmatic Elders stood
In slack-jawed wonder, the promise
of family, prosperity, and generations.

small wonder he choose the latter; he was a sensible man, and took his miracles as he found them.

The Astronomer

Best I can say, it was meant a distraction.
If the youngest son won't go into the Church
and if there's money enough that he needn't, well
who's to object to load of glass circles, and queer gears,
hauled to the South Tower and heaped about the floor?

'Long as Mr. Bertram's not drinking, like his brother,
or tupping the maids, Master and Mistress let him get about
to all sorts of nonsense, and no harm done, not at first.

Old Gregory and his boy, to help him heave about—
he's happy as a pig in cream, our boy.
Gregory grumbled , but his young 'un was all for the work:
soon mad for it as Master Bertie himself.

I say, let them at their fun.
I say, keeps the boys out of trouble, but don't mind me.

Problem came when he took to drawing
those pictures of the Moon. At first—
just a gray pebble, same as anyone saw,
then them bumps and holes, like the pox on white skin.

Still his Lordship didn't fret, for even then
those men came from London, with their books and maps,
staring through young Master's contraption
like children with a new toy.

But then he said he could see the Moon

closer than any else could—he drew forests,
with dreadful trees, and eyes. It was the eyes gave me the shivers
when I saw—peeping between, beneath broad leaves.
And buildings like the fripperies in the garden, half torn down.
And he said the bones of those that once lived there
moldered between the roots.
The men from London stopped coming
And Old Greg spat and grinned
and when they found Young Master baying
on the moor, beneath a full moon,
saying that they were watching,
and he could see them with bare eye
they took his contraptions apart
and bundled out the window
and sent Master Bertie abroad.

Gregory's boy wept a sevenday
until his Da cuffed it out of him.

Egyptology

One mustn't over-educate a woman:
it corrupts her essential purity of spirit,
that feminine, apart from womanhood,
as a shining pearl in the hot muck
of a farm midden: it's a separate thing, that once
crushed, corrupted, can never be unsullied—
therefore guard it well.

That's what Professor Travers says
expansive in the dining room over cigars
when the ladies have withdrawn.
Professor Travers is a respectable man,
heavy with learning and a beard,
and so the young men—a few promising
students, his solicitor, an artist of good family—
nod politely over their brandy
(although one or two of the most callow

spare a lingering thought for young Mrs. Travers—
fresh, dewy, graceful, the Spring of May/December
quiet, shy, with downcast eyes, and pert bosom: the artist
would like to paint her).

Professor Travers teaches his wife
to pronounce the hieroglyphs—but not to understand,
for that is unwise (remember that pearl, that midden),
like Milton's daughters, reading Greek
in soft accents that pleased their sire,
but not given to know what they are saying.

But knowledge is like a weed
That splits the well-made paving
of Men's Cities. Understanding comes,
subtle and ineluctable as a snake in the garden,
and she reads the tales of Set and Osiris,
Isis searching and Horus her son,
and smaller tales: love between the reeds,
teasing a lover, the small pang of pure pain

as a mother cradles a stillborn child
in a plain mud room.

And it seems to her, in those sweet hours
she can snatch alone when she is retired
for the night and the good professor is
entangled in his studies late, and leaves her be
and might even fall asleep over his books and scrolls
and a half-sleep paralyzes her limbs—
that a strange beast slips into her room
creeps between the sheets and nuzzles
behind her knees, touches
her belly, where understanding roots.

A lot like a jackal with a forked tail,
a little like a donkey, with ears made
by a drunken taxidermist,
with a smell like the scrape desert musk
and the tang of ants stirred up to war.

It tells her of mutilation and rebirth,
of catching songbirds in the reeds,

of showing a lover a new garment,
of betrayal, sorrow, honey and rich-scented wax.

Osiris lies re-riven in a velvet study,
Isis takes a carriage to Portsmouth
to catch a steamer for African shores,
on her thigh, a hand-shaped bruise,
not unlike the hieroglyph that denotes the sound—"d."

She wants to find the Birdcatcher's Daughter, see
on a tomb wall, a poem written
for the dead fetus of a child-queen, live
the tale of a Goddess digging through the rushes,

sullied.

How to Eat a Book

If you intend to read it
(why bother to eat
a book you haven't read?)
make sure you've finished each page
before you tear it away.

Spare some leaves between
the striped-branch spine
in case you've lost track
of the narrative.

Detach the page carefully,
or tear away the margins.
Wood-pulp paper is dry and sour;
cotton tastes the sweeter;
ink is always bitter.

Follow every second or third page
with a cherry
to soothe the taste from your tongue

After, your belly will hurt,
full of fruit and rhetoric
that's how you know
you've done it right.

Victory Garden
(For Peg Duthie)

some things are painful
catch you there, under the ribcage;
potent as the spear of God's ain true knight

the corgi, rummaging through the remains
of spring's glorious garden, snuffling
the rusty leaves, finding a forgotten courgette

more yellow than green, and tough
as your aunt, still ration-minded,
poor dear, in her mended stockings

you stand irresolute, holding the vegetable
too big to be obscene, a whisper short
of a newborn's weight, and listen

to small things, rustling in the overgrowth
what to make of this object, still vibrating
steamed into compliance, or pickled

or baked into bread, or wasted marvel
of this century, paling like a cast-off knight
or movie star upon your countertop

now you notice the cur is old, white
about the muzzle and the nails too long
and the spraddle that tells of sore hips

he looks up at you and grins, still the fairy steed
and all of Arthur's knights that lived to feel
the cold in their bones, sitting `round you in the sun

some things are painful, sweet
and catch you there.

After the Crash

Faith is the substance of things hoped for, she read,
in something called *Hebr* that flickered in transient pixels
on the star-cracked handscreen.

Faith was the name of the ship,
Substance came in sealtubes,
but *Hope* had no referent.

The tanks and their inhabitants waited, patient,
while she relearned: CO_2 levels, sugar absorption,
polymer flex, surface tension, photosynthesis, toxins.

'Tween times, tired, she rifled the pulpy fragments
of burned, water-logged books, piecing them like puzzles:
Dic ens; J Eyr; Persuas—in search of this thing called Hope.

Emily said, *Hope is the thing with feathers*,
Charlotte said, *Hope to meet again there*, meaning heaven, when nothing else
        remained,
while Jane said that women loved, *when existence or when Hope is gone*.

She drained the tanks and the web-fingered,
bubble-headed creatures grew,
while she grew old.

She told them tales of Adam and his consort, Anne
And monsters in the attic that might be tamed, might eat
Substance from your hand.

And of the angel Eyr, Hope
(in the Old Speech) who waits, wingspread,
watching the sea, watching, faithful, for the fleet, and rescue.

After she died, none knew what *Rescue* meant
(although it was a power-word); they kept it, because
like Hope, it was precious to her.

Ghost Feet

Old photographs are deceptive,
so peaceful-seeming. Black-clad workmen,
factory girls in white eyelet,
shopkeepers leaning in their doorways,
a dog asleep in the sun.

Each day's a séance, and we don't see
eager ectoplasm pressing upon us
seeking entrance at every orifice:
silent mouth. Deafened ear.

In that frail, persistent,
silver-speckled medium
we see a spiritual fabric:
movement too quick
for the languorous film to capture.
An army of ghost feet,

churning through the muddy Chinatown streets
like a turbulent stream. Marching
down a decorous sidewalk,
before hotels of Empire, or townhouses,
standing corseted, cheek by jowl.

Or here, a high-buttoned shoe
the leg in its black stocking,
fading upwards, terminating
as if tibia and fibula were severed.

Here's the honesty of this photograph:
the foot, lighting like a grasshopper,
and further on a child, seeming still—
but look closer. She blurs—
not going right or left, or back or forth,
but vibrating like a molecule.

The child, the feet, the men, the girls,
the dog, bound in cloth and leather and silver—

going somewhere—
anywhere.

1859 California St., [Washington, D.C.]
Library of Congress, Prints & Photographs Division,
LC-DIG-npcc-30268 (digital file from original)

Acknowledgments

"Veritas Was a Maid in the House of Forever," *Anemone Sidecar*, February 2006.

"Hepatocellular Cancer, Stage Four," *Chizine*, July 2006.

"Cabazon," *Strange Horizons*, August 2005.

"Hero," *Ideomancer*, September 2006.

"Hungry: Some Ghost Stories," *Lone Star Stories*, April 2008.

"The Passion," *Neverary*, April 2005.

"Reptile Brain," *Lone Star Stories*, June 2005.

"Every Thirty Years on Cygnus 5," *Lone Star Stories*, October 2005.

"The Miracle of the Gulls, 1848," *Dreams and Nightmares*, Issue 74.

"Egyptology," *Mythic Delirium*, Issue 21.

"After the Crash," *The Sword Review*, June 2006.

About the Author

Samantha Henderson lives in Covina, California by way of England, South Africa, Illinois and Oregon. Her poetry has been published in *Strange Horizons*, *Goblin Fruit*, *Weird Tales*, *Sporty Spec*, *Dreams and Nightmares*, *Mythic Delirium*, *Jabberwocky*, *Astropoetica* and *Stone Telling*, and she is the co-winner, with Kendall Evans, of the 2010 Rhysling Award for speculative poetry for "In the Astronaut Asylum." Her fiction has been reprinted in *The Year's Best Fantasy and Science Fiction*, *Steampunk II: Steampunk Reloaded*, and *The Mammoth Book of Steampunk*. She is the author of the Ravenloft novel *Heaven's Bones* and the Forgotten Realms novel *Dawnbringer*, and is the editor of *inkscrawl*, the magazine of short speculative poetry. For more information, please see her website at http://www.samanthahenderson.com.

www.ingramcontent.com/pod-product-compliance
Lightning Source LLC
Chambersburg PA
CBHW050916120626
46552CB00004B/1597